Grumpy Bear

Best Friend Bear

Secret Bear

This book belongs to:

Wish Bear

Love-a-lot Bear

Published by Scholastic Inc.
90 Old Sherman Turnpike, Danbury, CT 06816.

SCHOLASTIC and associated logos are trademarks and/or registered trademarks of Scholastic Inc.

ISBN 0-439-79993-7

First Scholastic Printing, October 2005

Care Bears™
Friendship Club
Cheer Up!

by
Quinlan B. Lee

Illustrated by
Warner McGee

SCHOLASTIC INC.

New York   Toronto   London   Auckland   Sydney
Mexico City   New Delhi   Hong Kong   Buenos Aires

Poor Bedtime Bear was not feeling well.
Cheer Bear found him tucked in his bed.

"What's wrong?"
Cheer Bear asked.

"My nose is stuffy and my head hurts," Bedtime
Bear replied. "How will I watch over everyone tonight?"
"Cheer up," said Cheer Bear. "I'll take care
of everything."

That night, while everyone was getting ready for bed, Cheer Bear gathered all the wishing stars together.

"I'll be staying up tonight so Bedtime Bear can get some extra rest," she told the stars.

"Let's go tuck in everyone and say good night."

9

The next morning, Cheer Bear
was very tired. She was just dozing off,
when Share Bear bumped into her.

"I am so sorry," said Share Bear. "I was in such a hurry, I didn't see you."

"That's okay," said Cheer Bear. But why are you in a hurry? You look very worried."

"The Care Bear Cousins are coming to Care-a-lot Castle for a party tonight," said Share Bear. "I still have to bake the cake and make the decorations. There is so much to do!"

"Cheer up," said Cheer Bear. "I'll help you. I can make that cake in two shakes."

"Aren't you tired?"
asked Share Bear.

"Don't worry. I could make a cake with my eyes closed," teased Cheer Bear.

13

Cheer Bear worked hard to make the cake
for the party. But she was so sleepy, she didn't notice
how much batter she was making.

"This cake should be just enough for all the Care Bear Cousins," she said. She rubbed her tired eyes.

"And now I have just enough time for a snooze before I need to frost it."

But just as Cheer Bear was putting the cake in
the oven, Wish Bear and Funshine Bear came by.
"You look so sad," Cheer Bear told them.
"What's wrong?"

"We wish we could cheer up Grumpy Bear," Wish Bear replied.

"But it isn't working. What fun is that?" added Funshine Bear.

"Cheer up," said Cheer Bear.
"I'm the Care Bear to do it!
Come on!
Let's go make happiness happen!"

17

In the car on the way to see Grumpy
Bear, Cheer Bear yawned and yawned.
"We're almost there," said Wish Bear.

"Great," said Cheer Bear. "Because I still need to finish that cake in two . . . in two . . ."

"Shakes?" finished Funshine Bear. But when he turned around, Cheer Bear was fast asleep.

ZZZZZZZZZZZ

Cheer Bear slept
all afternoon.

ZZZZZZZZZZZZ ZZ

When she finally woke up, she was
back in Care-a-lot Castle, and the Care Bear
Cousins were already there for the party.

"Oh no," Cheer Bear cried.
"I didn't finish the cake."

"Cheer up,"
said Funshine Bear.
"We finished the cake
for you."

"And helping finish
the cake sure cheered
me up," said Grumpy
Bear. "It's just like you
always say, Cheer Bear:

'Nothing makes you feel happier
than helping a friend.'"

"And it was a good thing
we had help," said Share Bear.
"You made a gigantic cake.
It took all of us to frost it."

"Uh-oh," said Cheer Bear. "I made so much cake batter because I was so tired."

"Cheer up", said Share Bear. "You made enough cake for all the Care Bear Cousins and enough for me to share with all the Care Bears. Now come on, it's party time!"

Cheer Bear smiled as she looked around
at all of her friends enjoying the party. "I only
wish Bedtime Bear was feeling better and could
be here," she sighed.

"Did you say *wish*?" asked Wish Bear.

Just then Bedtime Bear popped out
from behind a cloud. "Cheer up", he cried.

"Because here I am!"

"You're here!" said Cheer Bear.
"You must be feeling better."

"I sure am," said Bedtime Bear.
"Thanks to you, I'm feeling a lot better."
"Thanks to you," said Share Bear.
"We're *all* feeling a lot better."

"No one's better
at cheering us up than
you are, Cheer Bear,"
said Secret Bear.

"Three cheers for Cheer Bear!"

"But I almost messed everything up," said Cheer Bear.

"Cheer Bear, we would love you even if you did mess up," said Wish Bear. "But it all turned out great! Because messing up is kind of like a rainy day."

"Just add a little sunshine,"

said Funshine Bear. "And what do you get?"

Everyone looked down at
Cheer Bear's tummy. "A rainbow!"
all the Care Bears cried.

"Cheerific!"

laughed Cheer Bear.

35

How Can You Be Cheerful Like Cheer Bear?

Bedtime Bear, Share Bear, and Grumpy Bear were feeling badly.

- ❤ Do you ever feel that way?
- ❤ When?

Cheer Bear helped her friends feel better.

- ❤ Who helps you feel better when you need cheering up?
- ❤ Do you know someone you could help feel better?
- ❤ What could you do to make that person smile?

Cheer Bear made some mistakes while she was trying
to help her friends.

- ❤ Did her mistakes turn out okay in the end?
- ❤ Have you ever made a mistake that turned out to be okay?
- ❤ Who loves you, even when you make a mistake?

Bashful Heart Bear

Cheer Bear

Share Bear

Bedtime Bear

Funshine Bear